Beast Quest®

PETROK THE STONE WARRIOR

BY ADAM BLADE

THE NEW PROTECTORS!

Welcome to the world of Beast Quest!

When a series of Beast attacks shocked the peaceful land of Tangala, Queen Aroha called for a worthy Master or Mistress of the Beasts. But one fighter wasn't enough for the grave danger the kingdom faced, and four candidates pledged their weapons to the Queen to restore peace. There is strength in unity and power in friendship. Together, Katya from the Forest of Shadows, Nolan of Aran, Miandra from the western shore and Rafe of Doran will venture to new lands and battle enemies of the realm. The fate of Tangala is in their hands.

*While there's blood in their veins,
the New Protectors will never
give up the Quest…*

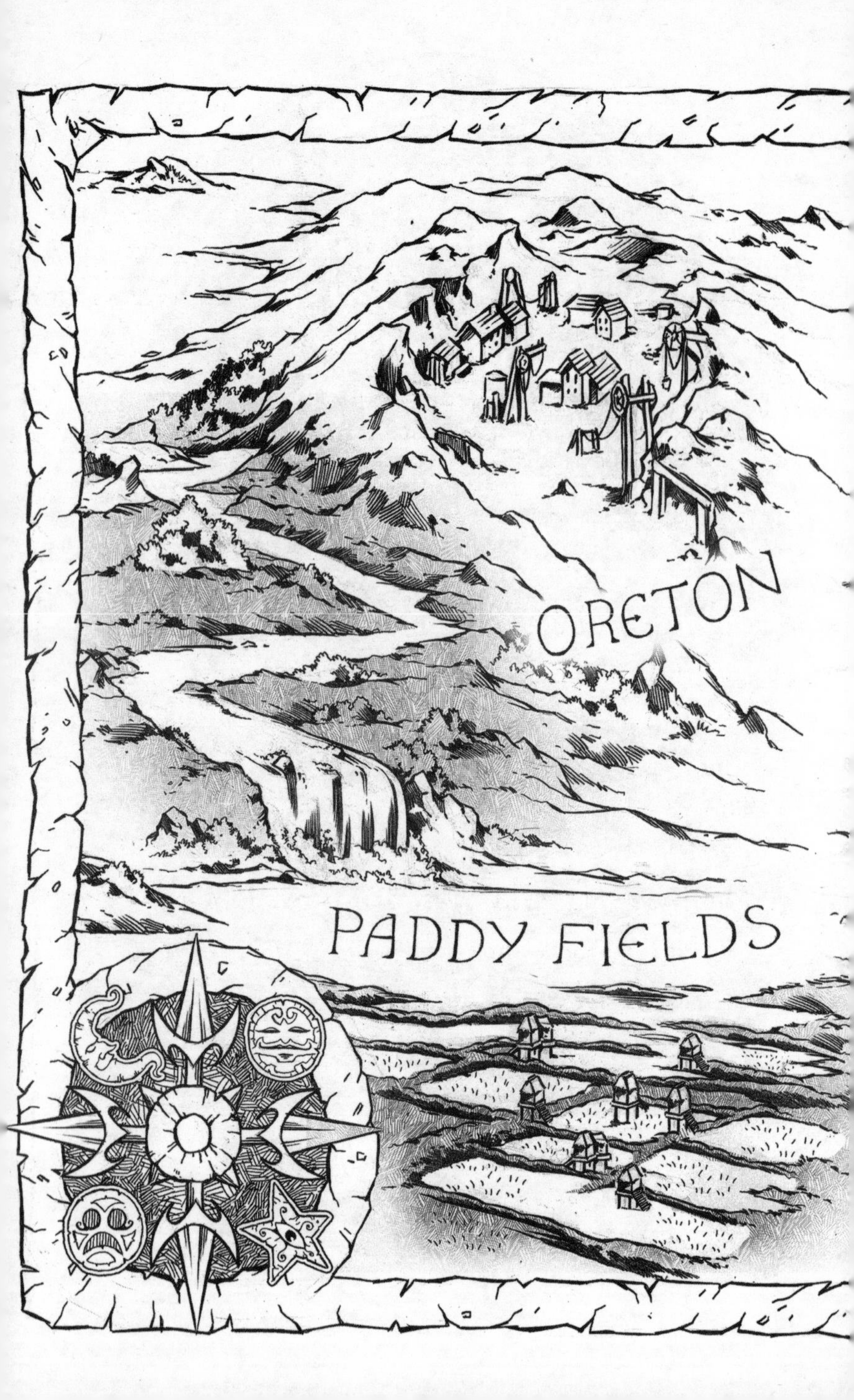
ORETON
PADDY FIELDS

TANGALA
PANIA
ARAN

There are special gold coins to collect in this book. You will earn one coin for every chapter you read.

Find out what to do with your coins at the end of the book.

CONTENTS

Our brave heroes are victorious!

The Beasts are vanquished, the kingdom safe once more. At long last we have bidden farewell to noble Tom and Elenna, and they have returned in triumph to Avantia.

Yet still a darkness clouds my mind, which is why I have remained in Tangala.

Day and night I pore over the dusty scrolls, seeking answers. A strange magic has tainted the weapons of the New Protectors. They crackle and glow with a mysterious purple light. They pulse with power.

What it means, I know not. But, for the sake of Tangala, I will uncover the truth. The kingdom must be protected, even if that means meddling with dangerous sorcery, long forgotten and forbidden...

Daltec

BURIED ALIVE

Compared to the moonlit woodland Nolan had just left, the jungle around him felt like a steamy kitchen. He was still dizzy from travelling through Daltec's portal, and sweat trickled down his spine. In the muggy gloom beneath the trees, Marilla crouched beside a small, green pond, lapping thirstily. Nolan watched, taking in the werewolf's lithe frame and shaggy coat. He could hardly believe she was really going to be his new

companion, helping him defeat Beasts in his role as a Protector of Tangala.

This is going to take some getting used to! he thought. Marilla turned, fixing Nolan with a steady gaze. The wolf's amber eyes were shot through with glimmers of orange and gold which shone like the embers of a fire.

"*You should not stare,*" Marilla growled, her words forming directly in Nolan's mind.

Nolan flushed even hotter. "I-I-I'm sorry," he stammered.

Marilla's gaze softened, becoming

almost gentle. "*I did not intend to shame you*," she said. "*You will never have seen anyone like me before. When the Metamorphia created me, back when they were still a force for good, they made no others*."

"I'm still sorry," Nolan said. "And I'm glad you're here!"

"*As am I*," Marilla said. She turned from the pool and stretched, arching her back and extending her arms so Nolan could see each powerful claw. "*I have been a prisoner for far too long*," she added. Marilla, along with three other mystical creatures created in ancient times by the sorcerers known as the Metamorphia, had been trapped in stone for longer than Nolan could imagine. Daltec, the Avantian wizard, had freed the creatures so that they could serve as companions to Nolan and his three friends, the other New Protectors of Tangala. But only moments later, an evil sorceress called Zuba had appeared and conjured four Evil Beasts of her own, sending them to different corners of the kingdom. Now it was the New Protectors' job to track down and defeat those Beasts with the help of their otherworldly companions.

Marilla lifted her great, shaggy head and sniffed the humid air. "*I can sense no trace of a Beast yet*," she said. "*We must begin our hunt*."

Nolan peered into the dense, dark vegetation all around them. Glossy leaves and giant ferns dripped with moisture on every side, and hairy loops of vine hung down from the canopy above. The broad trunks of the trees were lichen-furred and the air was so thick with the stench of decaying vegetation that it was hard to breathe. Nolan could hear the soft patter of water all around him, but otherwise the jungle was ominously still. With no obvious path in sight, he pointed to a narrow opening between two massive ferns.

"I guess this way is as good as any," he said.

Marilla dipped her head. "*You lead and I will follow*," she answered. Nolan lifted his scythe and strode into the undergrowth. After only a few paces, he was forced to swing his blade, hacking a path through the stems and vines. Marilla fell into place behind him, her eyes burning brightly as she scanned the shadows beneath the trees. Knowing a Beast waited somewhere in the gloom, Nolan was very grateful for her presence.

Despite the sticky heat, Nolan quickly fell into a rhythm, chopping and slicing through bushes and ferns. Sweat soon drenched his tunic and his arms ached, but in a good way. He was used to this kind of work. Back on his father's farm, he had spent many long days harvesting corn with his scythe. That seemed a lifetime ago.

"*You are strong*," Marilla said, her deep voice warm with approval.

Nolan smiled a little sadly. “It’s more about technique than strength. I was always smaller and weaker than my brothers, so my mother taught me to use skill instead of force.”

"*She sounds like a wise woman,*" Marilla said.

A pang of sorrow caught in Nolan's throat. "She was," he managed at last. "She died when I was eight, so I grew up with just my father and older brothers."

"*I am sorry to hear that,*" Marilla said, softly. The wolf paused, and when she spoke again her voice sounded wistful. "*What is it like to have a family?*" she asked.

Nolan frowned, considering her question. "Good in a lot of ways," he said. "But difficult too. My mother always knew what to say when my brothers teased me. I still miss her."

"*I am sure she would be proud if she could see you now*," Marilla said. Then her tone changed sharply. "*Wait!*" she hissed. Nolan turned to see the wolf's eyes narrow and her fur bristle as she sniffed the air. "*I smell danger...*"

Nolan caught a whiff of something too – almost like rotten eggs but with a bitter edge that smelled... unnatural. *Like one of Daltec's spells, gone wrong.*

"*We must be on our guard*," Marilla told him. Nolan started off again, but after just a few more paces, the stench grew so bad his nostrils stung and his eyes smarted. Suddenly, with a wild clap of wing-beats, a flock of colourful birds exploded up from the undergrowth, fleeing skywards. A troop of monkeys scrambled past, screeching as they tore through the trees. The whole jungle had come alive with the panicked flaps and scrabbling paws of countless birds and small animals, all bolting in terror. A moment later, they were gone and silence fell.

Nolan froze, his senses thrumming. The sweltering jungle

felt stiller than ever after the commotion, but the quiet was tense and heavy, as if even the trees were holding their breath. Marilla growled softly. "*I do not like this place*," she said.

Nolan raised his scythe once more, as much to defend himself as to cut a path. But as he and Marilla pushed further into the undergrowth, nothing stirred. The only sound was the ***SNICK*** and ***CHOP*** of Nolan's blade.

Though they met no more jungle creatures, the stench that filled the air got stronger and stronger, making Nolan's head ache. He soon found himself swaying on his feet. His vision began to spin and he blinked hard, nausea rising in his throat. Staggering a few more paces, Nolan shook his head, trying to clear the dizziness, but then his foot hit a tangle of roots and he pitched forwards, almost toppling.

"*Careful,*" Marilla said. "*Do you need to stop?*"

Nolan shook his head. "It's just that terrible smell," he said. "We need to keep going. Those animals were fleeing from something, so we must be on the right track."

Marilla nodded in agreement, though her eyes were clouded with worry. "*We need to get you away from whatever is causing this stench.*"

Nolan lifted his scythe again, grateful for the tingle of power that flowed into his arm. The blade had been infused with magical strength granted by the power of Tom's enchanted gauntlet. Its newly golden edge reminded Nolan of why he was here. *I am a Protector of Tangala!* he told himself. *It is my duty to defeat whatever awaits us, using the skills taught to me by Tom, Master of the Beasts*. But though he stood taller, his head still swam.

As Nolan stumbled onwards, slashing and slicing with his scythe, he found himself grunting with each stroke, his arm burning and his skin slick with sweat. The woody stems and clinging tendrils all around him seemed to be getting denser the further he went.

Cold sweat beaded Nolan's skin, but he forced himself to keep going, focussing on each weary step, sucking in putrid air. His world had narrowed to a suffocating tunnel of dank, clutching vegetation, and his feet felt numb, like blocks of wood.

He frowned, trying to think... His pulse thumped in his ears and his head throbbed with pain. "*Nolan?*" a deep voice growled. It seemed to come from far away.

As he staggered onwards, Nolan caught a glimpse of something blue up ahead, something familiar that made his heart clench. *Mother!* He'd recognise her blue dress anywhere! Squinting hard, Nolan could just make out his mother's trim frame, her long plait of dark hair...but she was moving away from him, into darkness.

"Wait!" Nolan cried, but his voice

came out as a croak. He broke into a stumbling run, crashing through ferns, mud sucking at his boots as he staggered. “Mother!” he called. *I have to reach her!* His breath heaved and bile burned his throat. Tepid water sloshed around his ankles, then his shins, but he forged onwards, every step harder than the last. Suddenly, the ground beneath him gave way completely. Nolan’s stomach dropped like a stone as he sank into deep mud first to his knees, then to his waist. He reached out desperately, trying to grab a branch, to catch hold of

something...anything! But the slimy mud sucked him down, swallowing him whole, squeezing the breath from his lungs. Nolan took one last desperate gasp, terror burning through him, then the mud closed over his head, entombing him in darkness – burying him alive.

DANGER
1

PANTHER ATTACK!

Blood thundered in Nolan's ears as panic flooded his veins. He tried to struggle, but the sticky mud held his body fast and he couldn't move. Already, his lungs burned. Mud filled his nostrils and oozed between his tightly closed lids. *I'm going to die!* he realised. *Mother, please help!*

Suddenly, Nolan felt pressure at his wrist – a sharp, nagging pain, then a tug. *Mother*, he wondered, *is that you?* The tugging grew stronger and more insistent, the pain clearing his muddled thoughts.

Mother's gone...dead, he remembered. *It must be Marilla! She's trying to pull me free!* Drawing his scattered senses together, Nolan focussed on holding his breath and forcing his panic down, slowing his pounding heart.

The powerful teeth gripping his arm tugged steadily, but Nolan could feel the mud that encased him resisting Marilla's strength, fighting against her. *She can't do this alone. I have to help.*

Nolan racked his brains and remembered something his mother had told him about quicksand. *Don't panic. Small movements. Start with your legs.* With Marilla's powerful jaws still pulling his arm, Nolan wriggled his feet. *I hope mud works the same way as quicksand!*

At first, Nolan could only twitch the toes of his boots up and down, but before long, he could move his whole feet. He felt some of the terrible sucking pressure of the mud around his ankles loosen. He wriggled again, this time moving his lower legs, flexing the muscles. Cool water oozed into the tiny spaces his movements created, and the slime began to loosen its grip. Bit by painful bit, Marilla pulled Nolan upwards. His lungs shuddered for air, but he twisted his torso and jerked his limbs. *Don't breathe yet!* he told himself, knowing that deadly mud would flood his lungs if he did.

Just as Nolan began to think his lungs would burst, Marilla gave one mighty tug and his head broke the surface. Heaving a massive gulp of air, Nolan blinked the sludge from his eyes. Marilla was right beside him, her forepaws braced against a fallen branch and her powerful shoulders straining. Nolan managed to free his other arm and pushed it flat against the surface of the swamp, adding his strength to Marilla's. His upper body slid from the mud, then his legs, and finally, he was free. He lay panting and gasping, covered in filth, but filled

with joy to still be alive.

"*Are you well?*" Marilla asked.

"Thanks to you!" Nolan said. He gingerly eased his way across the mud on his belly until he was back on firm ground. "I saw my mother..." he said, but then trailed off, frowning. "But that doesn't make sense. I must have been dreaming, or hallucinating."

"*Petrok*," Marilla said, the word weighted with dread.

"What?" Nolan asked.

"*A giant ape that used to live in the Dark Jungle in a lair protected by noxious marshes*," Marilla said. "*The gas from the marshes caused people to see things, making them easy prey*."

"But why only me?" Nolan asked, doing his best to scrape the stinking mud from his face.

"*I'm not sure*," Marilla answered. "*Maybe I am protected because I am a mystical being. You should wrap some cloth around your mouth and nose to keep the worst of the gases out.*"

Nolan looked down at his mud-caked tunic and grimaced. But Marilla was right. He tore a strip from the hem then tied it around his face, shuddering at the clammy touch of the material. It stank of rotting vegetation, but anything was better than the toxic gas – or the pain of seeing his mother again. He stood, shrugging away the cold horror that still clung to him.

"Let's go!" he said, grimly. "We have a Beast to defeat."

Nolan led the way, cutting a path

with his scythe once more. His sodden tunic chafed his skin, and it was even harder to breathe with his face wrapped in cloth, but it was working – he didn't see any more visions. He pressed on through the stifling heat, ignoring the ache in his arm and the burning sweat that stung his eyes.

After what seemed like an age, the vines and vegetation finally thinned, then parted to reveal a clearing. Blinking in the sudden sunlight, Nolan straightened his aching back. At the centre of the space, half covered in moss and creepers, stood a colossal sand-coloured structure. The building had a wide, square base, then rose to a triangular peak. A vast flight of crumbling steps led up to a gaping entrance at the front, which was flanked on either side by a pair of cracked stone plinths. With weeds sprouting from the cracks, the badly worn building looked far older than anything Nolan had encountered before. A solemn stillness crept over him.

"*A ziggurat*," Marilla growled, thoughtfully, gazing at the half-ruined building. "*It is an ancient*

place of worship. A temple."

The air in the sunlit clearing seemed fresher than the jungle, so Nolan cautiously pulled the mask from his face, letting it sit lower on his neck. The smell was gone. Stepping towards the temple, he spotted weathered lines scored into the sandstone, almost covered by lichen and moss.

"I think this is some kind of mural," he told Marilla, then he began to carefully scrape the moss away with his scythe. The first etchings he uncovered depicted a giant ape-like creature clutching a screaming person in each great fist. Further along the wall, the carvings showed people kneeling on the ground in front of the same Beast, offering baskets of food and drink. In the final picture, the huge ape was holding a whole tree in each hand, the trunks crossed like a pair of swords. *Petrok*, Nolan realised. He shuddered.

"Why would Zuba want to resurrect something so terrible?" Nolan murmured.

Marilla, standing at his elbow, spoke gruffly, making him jump. "*The Metamorphia were once kindly and wise, but in the end they became consumed with rage. They wanted only to destroy Tangala. If Zuba is indeed the last of their line, she will be bent on the kingdom's destruction."*

Hearing a low rumbling growl from above them, Nolan looked up, then froze. Silently, he put a hand on Marilla's fur and pointed. At the top of the steps, seated on the plinths to either side of the temple's dark entrance, a pair of

panthers had appeared. Their sleek fur shone like polished stone, as dark as coal under the baking sun. Great muscles bulged beneath their glossy black pelts, and their eyes blazed bright green, like emeralds lit from within.

Nolan blinked. "Are they real,

or am I hallucinating again?" he whispered to Marilla.

"*I see them too*," Marilla whispered. "*But they do not look natural. I imagine we will soon find out if they are real.*"

The panthers rose and stretched lazily, flexing each razor-sharp claw as they arched their spines, their green eyes fixed on Nolan and Marilla. Nolan swallowed, fear tightening his throat. *They're just jungle creatures*, he told himself. *Maybe enchanted. But they're not Beasts. They have no reason to attack.* Keeping his scythe lowered, he lifted a hand, palm outwards in a soothing gesture.

"We don't mean you any harm," he said, gently. "We are looking for Petrok."

Silently, the panthers stepped down from their plinths, every movement slow and terrible. They yawned widely, displaying gleaming white fangs. Then their green eyes narrowed, and their long tails twitched. Nolan's guts churned with fear as the creatures' blazing eyes bored into him, but he lifted his scythe and held his ground.

Suddenly, both panthers sprang

at once, launching themselves towards Nolan and Marilla with terrible, blood-curdling snarls.

LAIR OF BONES

Nolan's heart lurched as one of the giant cats hurtled towards him, its curved black claws extended. He threw himself to the ground. With a scream of fury, the panther soared over his head. Nolan heard Marilla let out a strangled yelp as the other panther barrelled into her. He rose, spinning to face his attacker, but his boot caught a half-buried brick and he stumbled. Nolan managed to turn the fall into a roll, flipping on to his back just in time to see his attacker leap again, arching above him with claws outstretched.

With little other choice, Nolan lifted his scythe with both hands, slicing for the cat's exposed underbelly. As the blow connected, he braced himself, expecting to feel the slash of the panther's claws. But instead, the creature exploded into a cloud of powdery dust that rained down on him. Rock dust filled his throat and eyes and he coughed and spluttered, relief washing through his body.

Nolan leapt to his feet, blinking the dust from his eyes. Marilla was on her back, tussling with the second panther as it snapped at her throat. Nolan leapt again, swinging his scythe down towards the panther's inky hide. His blade swished through the air, cutting the creature in two. It burst apart, showering Marilla with chips of stone. She scrambled up on to all fours and shook herself clean.

"*Thank you,*" Marilla said, once her fur had settled. Then she turned to survey the cats' dusty remains. "*Interesting. Not hallucinations, but not real either. They must have been created by the Metamorphia long ago.*"

Nolan nodded, lifting his eyes to the square doorway: an impossibly dark opening against the brightness of the sky. An uneasy chill crept over him, and he shivered despite the heat. "Then I guess that's where we need to go..." he said. Nolan drew himself up to stand tall, and with a deep breath he started to climb the cracked and uneven temple steps.

Even before he reached the doorway, Nolan caught a musty whiff of air from inside. He frowned, thinking about the marsh gas that had poisoned him, but this scent was very different – a stale animal fustiness, something like rotting meat.

"Do you think the Beast lives inside here?" he asked Marilla. "The ceiling's high enough."

Marilla lifted her muzzle, her nose twitching. "*It certainly smells like a lair of some kind.*"

Nolan's skin tightened with dread.

"Then we must be ready to fight," he said. Raising his scythe, Nolan stepped into the ziggurat. He found himself in a lofty passageway with a high arched ceiling. If anything, the dusky space was even hotter than outside and the stench almost made him gag. He hurriedly tugged his makeshift face mask up over his nose. Ahead, the vast passageway led into darkness.

Marilla padded softly at Nolan's side, on all fours at first, then standing. They crept along the passage, the darkness growing deeper with each stride. Nolan strained his eyes, staring into the blackness all around him, wishing he had anything he could use to make a torch. Soon, the dark was so complete, he couldn't even see his own feet. Instead, his hearing seemed heightened so that his own shuffling footsteps echoed far too loudly in the hollow space. His skin tingled and shivers of fear ran up and down his spine. Every moment, he expected to run into something or to feel claws grab him from behind... He stopped dead, too terrified to move. *What kind of a hero am I?* he wondered. *Too afraid to walk in the dark...*

"*Put out your hand,*" Marilla said from his side. "*I will lead you.*"

Nolan felt the wolf's warm weight press against his leg. He let out a breath. "Thank you," he said. Then, with his hand on Marilla's coat, he set off once again.

Although the building had looked enormous from outside, the inside seemed even bigger. Nolan kept expecting the dark passage to end, but it just went on and on. Finally, he saw a faint glimmer of light up ahead. He quickened his pace, and the corridor soon opened into a great square chamber with a great chunk of stone missing from the roof. Shafts of sunlight fell through the hole, catching glittering motes of dust, and illuminating a colossal stone chair.

It took Nolan's eyes a few

moments to adjust to the light. All around the chair lay bones – big ones snapped in half, as if something had devoured the marrow, and small ones picked almost clean. He made out ribcages and grinning skulls, the antlers of deer and the horns of sheep. Piles of bones.

"How big did you say Petrok was again?" Nolan asked Marilla, trying to keep the quiver from his voice. But before Marilla could answer, a shadow fell over them. He looked up, and saw that something huge had blocked the hole in the roof, allowing in only a few slender fingers of light. It took Nolan a moment to understand what he was looking at, and then, his blood ran cold. A vast bloodshot eye was peering down at him from a leering ochre-coloured ape-like face.

PETROK'S THRONE

A tremendous roar, like the ***BOOM*** of thunder, filled the chamber, making the walls shudder and the floor quake. Nolan dropped into a crouch to keep from falling, and clapped his hands over his ears. Even Marilla hunkered down as the shaking went on and on, loosening chunks of stone from the ceiling which crashed to the ground below. The eye in the roof vanished, and for a moment, the light returned but then, with a terrific crash, a huge fist slammed down through the roof, widening the hole. A gigantic, red-brown form followed it, vaulting through the gap, bringing down chunks of brickwork. Sunlight flooded the chamber, and Nolan staggered back, watching in horror as an enormous gorilla-like creature landed on the stone chair.

Nolan swallowed hard and

Marilla growled, her teeth bared and her fur bristling. Petrok glared down at them, gnashing yellow teeth like slabs of stone. A carved helmet made of rock covered the upper part of his face, decorated with a glowing green jewel that was very like the green of the

panthers' eyes. The Beast wore a wide leather belt adorned with more green jewels, while the rest of his muscular body was covered in wiry red-brown hair – all except his fists, which were grey like his helmet, and seemed to be made of stone.

Nolan brandished his weapon, but then let it fall to his side. *To Petrok, it must look like a toothpick!* The Beast growled, a deep bass note that filled the room, making the walls and floor shudder and bringing more chips of rock raining down. Marilla growled in return, her eyes flashing like fire, then she crouched, ready to pounce.

"No!" Nolan cried. "The Beast's too big!" But Petrok roared as Nolan spoke, drowning out his voice. Marilla sprang, launching herself towards the Beast's throat, her teeth bared in a snarl. *I have to help her!* Nolan threw himself into his own attack, charging towards Petrok's throne. But before he had covered half the distance, Petrok's hairy arm shot out, swiping at Marilla.

Horror knifed through Nolan's gut as the Beast's stone fist careered towards his wolf companion. But somehow she managed to twist her body in mid-flight, arching her back and dodging the strike. Petrok's mighty fist slammed into a wall instead, smashing a hole with a thud. Light glanced through in dusty shafts as more shattered brickwork tumbled down in a deadly avalanche. A chunk of masonry hit Nolan's shoulder, making his arm fizz with pain. Another cracked him on the head. Choking dust filled the air, but he could still just make out Petrok, sitting on his throne, readying his fist for another strike. Back on her paws, Marilla turned to Nolan, her dense fur caked with dust. For the first time, Nolan saw fear in her eyes.

"*Run!*" she cried. "*This place is collapsing*." Without looking back, Marilla bounded towards the door, which was already half blocked with rubble.

Nolan raced after her, sprinting back the way they had come. Chunks of the ceiling thundered down around them. Nolan plunged headlong through the chaos and noise, dodging falling masonry, his boots pounding over the juddering floor.

"*Faster!*" Marilla roared, her panicked voice loud in Nolan's mind. He put on a frantic burst of speed, his heart thumping so hard it felt like it might leap from his chest. He could see the clearing up

ahead now – just a few more steps... Suddenly the crashes behind him rose to a thunderous roar. A howl of dusty wind slammed into Nolan from behind and with a surge of terror, he threw himself forwards, bursting out into the sun.

Marilla was already there,

panting for breath, her fur caked in blood-streaked grime. Nolan turned just in time to see the ruined ziggurat collapse in on itself, sending up a billowing mushroom cloud. With a few last clatters and crashes, the remains of the fallen temple settled. Then all fell still.

Nolan bent double, his hands on his knees as he gasped and coughed, clearing the brick dust from his lungs. It was in his eyes too, and even up his nose. Marilla shook herself clean and Nolan saw blood welling from several deep grazes along her flank. He put his hand up to his own throbbing head and it came away sticky and red. But he was still here, and Petrok was gone.

"He's buried himself alive!" Nolan said, staring at the huge pile of rubble that had covered the Beast. "We did it!"

But even as the words left his mouth, Petrok's huge fist punched up out of the mound. Nolan leapt back, and Marilla growled as the Beast heaved himself from the heap of stone fragments, clambering free. He shook the grime from his coat. Nolan gaped at the sheer size of the Beast. Out in the open, Petrok's broad shoulders were level with the tree canopy beyond. With a furious snort, his burning gaze fell on Nolan.

Nolan lifted his scythe, scanning the Beast's tough hide for any sign of weakness. A wave of hopelessness crashed over him as Petrok balled his fist, snarling. Nolan's scythe felt like a toy, pathetically small, but he squared his shoulders. *If I'm going to die, I'll die fighting!* he thought. Summoning every shred of strength he had, along with the power Tom had bestowed on his weapon, Nolan drew back his blade, wielding it with both hands.

As the Beast swung his gigantic fist, Nolan gritted his teeth and braced his body, blocking with his scythe. Sparks flew and pain jolted up Nolan's arms as he staggered under the blow. Somehow he managed to keep hold of his weapon, but all strength and feeling seemed to have left his arms. Petrok swiped for Nolan again and Nolan blocked once more, but this time the scythe flew from his numb fingers. Defenceless,

Nolan looked for Marilla, but the wolf had vanished. A broad, sickly grin spread over Petrok's face and his dark eyes gleamed. Nolan gulped, sick with dread. His weapon was gone, and with it any final tatters of hope. *This is it*, Nolan thought. *I'm finished.*

Petrok raised his fist high, ready to crush Nolan's skull.

1

A BITTER FIGHT

Nolan braced himself for the end, his back straight and his eyes on Petrok's hideous grin. But just as the gigantic ape began to lower his fist, Petrok froze, his face contorting into a puzzled frown. With a grunt, Petrok turned his

head, and Nolan saw Marilla appear on the ape's shoulder, then sink her teeth into his hairy neck.

Snorting in pain, Petrok shrugged, trying to dislodge the wolf, but Marilla hung on with her teeth and claws, worrying at the Beast's thick hide. With another snort, Petrok reached up and swatted Marilla away like a fly. Nolan gasped in horror as the wolf landed hard among the piled remains of the temple and rolled, her body tumbling over the sharp rubble.

"Marilla!" Nolan cried. The wolf-woman staggered up, one paw hanging limply and blood welling from a gash on her head. As Petrok rounded on Marilla, Nolan leapt towards his scythe and grabbed it.

"Leave her alone!" Nolan shouted, brandishing his weapon. "She is not your enemy. Your fight is with me!" Petrok didn't turn. Instead, he bent over Marilla's bruised body and snatched her up, lifting her high in his stone fist, dangling her over his cavernous mouth.

He's going to eat her! Nolan's brain screamed in horror.

"Stop!" he cried. Petrok glanced over his shoulder, his eyes narrowing as they fell on Nolan. Nolan felt a flicker of hope. "Marilla was created by the Metamorphia, just like you were," he called. "You don't have to be Zuba's tool. You can be a force for good like Marilla!" Nolan could almost see the Beast's slow brain working. "Please..."

Nolan said. But after another moment's hesitation, Petrok snorted, saliva dripping from his lips, and turned his attention back to the wolf. With a hungry grunt, he opened his gigantic mouth once more, ready to bite Nolan's companion in two.

Marilla struggled, snapping her jaws at Petrok's fingers and twisting her body – but there was no escape. Nolan realised the only chance he had of saving his friend lay in his scythe's magical strength.

He drew back his weapon, feeling it pulse with warmth in his hand.

I'll only get one chance. This has to work! With his eyes on the fleshy part of the Beast's arm where it met his vast stone fist, Nolan took aim. The blade of his scythe was glowing now, and his arm tingled with power. Nolan could feel the magical energy of Tom's Golden Armour building inside him. But already, Petrok was lowering Marilla towards his gigantic maw...

Nolan gritted his teeth and flung his weapon. As it spun through the air, he held his breath, willing his aim to be true... The scythe bit deep into Petrok's wrist with a fleshy ***THUNK*** and lodged there. Howling in agony, the Beast let Marilla fall. She landed deftly on all fours, while Petrok stared at the scythe jutting from his injured wrist, his eyes bulging with fury.

Petrok roared again, his cry

filling the jungle, shaking the trees. Nolan slammed his hands over his ears, reeling in pain at the unbearable noise. Gripping the handle of Nolan's scythe, the Beast wrenched it from his flesh and tossed it aside. Blood spurted from the deep wound. Nolan felt a surge of hope, but then Petrok lowered his injured arm, groping for the green jewels in his belt. As he touched the stones they flickered, growing dimmer. At the same time, the flow of blood from Petrok's wound slowed, then stopped. Grunting with satisfaction, Petrok lowered his gaze, searching for his prey.

"*Into the jungle!*" Marilla called, limping hurriedly towards Nolan. The fur at her temple was matted with blood, but her eyes looked clear. They both turned and fled for the trees, ducking behind a broad trunk. Nolan cast a longing glance back at his scythe, but to reach it, he would need to pass Petrok. *No chance.* The Beast was already looking their way, his dark eyes narrowed with hatred.

"Are you all right?" Nolan asked Marilla.

"*I heal quickly,*" she said. "*But I*

don't know how much help I will be defeating the Beast. His hide is so thick, my teeth barely pierced it."

Nolan nodded. "My scythe worked better than I had hoped," he said. "But I've lost it now. I did notice something about the jewels on Petrok's belt. He used them to heal himself, and when he did, their light dimmed. I think they may be the source of his strength. Perhaps, if we can remove his belt, we'll have a better chance against him."

"*Easier said than done*," Marilla replied.

Petrok stomped towards them,

bellowing and snorting. As he neared their hiding place, his nostrils flared and he frowned, sniffing the air.

"Run!" Nolan cried as Petrok reached for the tree. Marilla leapt away, darting through the undergrowth. Nolan fled too, zigzagging through the jungle as a terrific cracking, popping sound rang out behind him. Glancing back, Nolan saw Petrok had torn the tree from the ground and was wielding it like a giant club, just like in the pictographs they'd seen. Nolan doubled his speed, running for his life, terror burning through him. He had never felt so small, or so defenceless.

How can I fight a Beast when I don't even have a weapon?

A MOTHER'S ADVICE

CRASH! The ground shuddered as Petrok slammed his makeshift club into the earth. Nolan almost stumbled but managed to keep going, splintered twigs raining down all around him. With another

BOOM, the jungle floor bucked even more violently, throwing Nolan down on to his hands and knees. He scrambled up and was off again, fuelled by the terror in his veins. Slaloming through the undergrowth, he ducked branches and leapt tangled roots, twigs and thorns tearing at his arms and face. More crashes and thuds rang out behind him, and he glanced back to see Petrok swinging his tree-club like an axe, smashing a path through the jungle. Nolan pushed himself to go faster, his lungs burning and the terrible crash of falling trees filling his ears. He only hoped Marilla was far enough away to avoid being crushed.

Bursting out through a clump of ferns, Nolan almost plunged headlong into the bog that had swallowed him earlier. Without slowing, he barrelled towards it, leaping at the last moment... ***SPLASH!*** He landed in soft mud on the far side of the swamp, yanked his boots free, and kept going. Terror fizzed through Nolan's body as he plunged onwards, and now he could feel his legs tiring and his lungs fighting for air. A furious, wordless bellow of rage shook the jungle behind him, and Nolan glanced back to see Petrok knee-deep in the bog, both feet stuck fast.

With a surge of relief, Nolan skidded to a stop and bent double, catching his breath with heaving gasps. In the swamp, the Beast struggled and roared, sinking deeper with each movement, still brandishing his tree. Marilla was nowhere to be seen, so Nolan decided to head back to the clearing. *With any luck she'll be there and I'll have time to get my scythe!*

Leaving a wide margin around the roaring, fuming Beast, Nolan sprinted back through the jungle. Apart from a few broken branches and tattered ferns, the way was clear now. Petrok had destroyed everything. Before long, Nolan reached the clearing to find Marilla there before him, standing guard over his scythe.

"Petrok's trapped!" Nolan told the wolf. But she shook her head.

"*Not any longer*," she said, glancing over Nolan's shoulder. His heart sank, and he turned, already knowing what he would see.

Petrok was storming back along the path he had cleared, dripping with mud and shaking his fist. He had let his club go, but looked angrier than ever.

Nolan sighed. "How can I possibly defeat a Beast so much bigger than me?" he said. Then he paused, thinking. His words had sparked a memory, and like dry tinder catching light, he had the glimmer of an idea.

"Of course!" he said.

"*What?*" Marilla asked.

Nolan grinned, a risky plan forming in his mind. "You remember how I told you my mother always gave me good advice?" he said.

The wolf-woman nodded.

"Well, when my brothers fought

me, she told me to use their size against them. It almost always worked. I don't need to run away from Petrok. I need to run *towards* him!"

Marilla shook her head firmly. "*This isn't the same...*" she said. But Nolan was already running at full speed towards the Beast.

Petrok's dark eyes gleamed as he saw Nolan racing back in his direction. His mouth spread into a wide, cruel grin and he licked his lips.

Nolan smiled in grim satisfaction. *You think you've already won...*

As Nolan closed in on the Beast, he could see a string of saliva dripping from Petrok's mouth. "I'm not the easy meal you think I am!" Nolan muttered. Petrok crouched low to the ground, planting his legs wide, then reached out for Nolan. The jewels on the Beast's helmet and belt pulsed with light. He gnashed his giant tombstone teeth hungrily, and Nolan had one last nagging doubt. *What if I'm wrong about the jewels?* But he shook the thought away. Petrok hooted with triumph, his hand descending to grab. But just as the Beast began to close his fist, Nolan threw himself into a skid, sliding beneath Petrok's arm and between his trunk-like legs. As soon as he was behind Petrok, Nolan turned and leapt, swinging his scythe high with both hands, aiming for the Beast's belt.

Nolan's blade hooked neatly on to the belt, and he yanked his weapon with all his strength. For a moment, he feared it wouldn't work. The handle of the scythe splintered with the force, but the thick leather of the belt split apart too. Petrok howled with fury and whirled around sharply as Nolan fell backwards. The gorilla's belt slid from his waist and hit the ground with a thud. Instantly, the bright green light that shone from the jewels flickered and went out. Not only that, but their green hue became darker, shifting to the bruised purple of a thundercloud.

Petrok towered over Nolan, glowering with fury, as he began to stand. The jewel in the Beast's helmet had turned purple too, but Petrok didn't seem any weaker. Nolan's burst of triumph was quickly replaced with a terrible, sinking dread. Petrok stamped one giant foot and the ground beneath them shook, hurling Nolan from his feet again and throwing him on to his back. His head slammed against the ground with a sickening crack, and his vision spun. He blinked hard to clear the dizziness, but as he tried to stand, the whole jungle whirled around him. Petrok leaned over Nolan so closely, Nolan could smell the rotten-meat stink of his breath. Petrok's dark eyes flashed with a victorious light, and he reached for Nolan.

Colossal rock fingers closed around Nolan's chest, crushing his ribs, squeezing the breath from his body. Lifting Nolan up until their eyes were level, the Beast grinned. Nolan's heartbeat faltered as he looked into the depths of Petrok's gaze and saw only cruelty and an animal lust for blood. Petrok squeezed harder. Nolan felt his ribs cracking. He gasped but there was no space in his lungs for a breath. Petrok growled, and the deep rumble shuddered through Nolan's body, making his insides quiver.

Staring into the Beast's hungry, pitiless gaze, Nolan knew it would be the last thing he ever saw.

But then he noticed the colour of Petrok's eyes shift. They seemed to cloud over, losing their fiery sheen, becoming empty and dead. The rumbling growl died in Petrok's throat, and Nolan realised the Beast's grip was weakening. He

could breathe again! Petrok had grown still. The Beast's face had changed colour from reddish-brown flesh to a matt, colourless grey that matched his eyes. *No...not just his face!* His whole body was grey – and completely lifeless.

The Beast had turned into a statue.

DANGER
1

TEAMWORK AND TRICKERY

Nolan squirmed in Petrok's grip, twisting his body and pushing against the cold, hard rock that trapped him. The Beast's stone fingers scraped his skin raw, but Nolan didn't care. He strained and heaved, grazing his knees and elbows, tearing his clothes until, little by little, he struggled free. Crawling from Petrok's hand and on to his wide stone arm, Nolan stood up. The jungle floor was far below.

Petrok's face had hardened into a deep, leering frown. His giant head rose above the tree canopy: a colossal statue, frozen in time.

I did it, thought Nolan. *I vanquished the Beast!*

"*Can you get down?*" Marilla called. She was standing on one of Petrok's stone feet, gazing up at him.

Nolan nodded. "Back home, I

used to climb trees sometimes
to get away from
my brothers.
This should
be much
easier." 
Petrok's
coarse
pelt, now
hardened
to stone,
made for
perfect
hand- and
footholds. Nolan
hurried back along

the length of Petrok's arm, then scrambled down on to the Beast's broad chest. From there, it didn't take long to reach the ground where Marilla waited.

"*Your mother would be very proud!*" Marilla said. "*Your skill with your weapon and quick thinking may just have saved Tangala!*"

Nolan sank to the ground beside Petrok's belt, his knees suddenly weak. His ribs burned with each breath and every part of his body ached, but he couldn't stop grinning. He spotted his scythe lying nearby, its handle broken in two, but even that didn't dim his joy. It could easily be mended.

"We did it together," he told Marilla. The wolf-woman looked as battered and worn as Nolan felt, but her eyes were bright and filled with pride.

From a tree nearby, a lone red and blue parrot flapped upwards, landing on top of Petrok's head. Following its path, Nolan's gaze fell on Petrok's helmet with its purple jewel, and he had a thought. "We will need to carry Petrok's belt back with us. Those jewels are powerful; we mustn't leave them here. It's a shame we can't take the one from his helmet."

Marilla nodded. "*It will be a long journey and a hard one, but we can take it in turns to carry the belt. A burden shared is a burden halved.*"

Nolan smiled. "We make a good team!"

The evening sun poured through the stained-glass windows of the banquet hall in Queen Aroha's palace, casting bright patterns on the table before Nolan. His plate was empty now, but the table still groaned with food, and dessert hadn't even been served yet. He let out a contented sigh. His wounds were starting to heal, and Marilla's were too. She sat across the table, gnawing on a huge leg of ham. Rafe, Katya and Miandra were seated around him, along with their magical companions, and all had a story of victory to tell.

Rafe offered a plump ripe grape to his wyvern friend Rugara, and she pecked it from his hand. Nolan grinned. Each of the New Protectors seemed to have formed a bond with their companion as close as the one he shared with Marilla.

The door at the far end of the hall banged open, and Prince Rotu strode through, still dressed in his riding cloak. "Hello, my friends!" the young prince boomed. "I hear we have much to celebrate! Congratulations, all of you. You have served your kingdom well."

Nolan leapt to his feet and his friends did the same, sketching quick bows to the prince.

"Don't stand!" Rotu said. "Please go back to your meal." He smiled, but then suddenly looked distracted, his brow furrowing as

he glanced around the table. "I was actually hoping to find that wizard," Rotu said. "He is not at your feast?"

"He is in his study," Rafe said,

flushing a little as he spoke. Nolan wondered if Rafe would ever get used to speaking to the royal family. He was still nervous around them, even now he was a hero.

"Yes!" Katya added, grinning. "Daltec unearthed some dusty stone tablets back at the Emperor's Temple in Saitang," she said. "Apparently, deciphering them couldn't wait." The ruined temple was where Daltec had freed Marilla and the other three mythical creatures that now feasted with Nolan and his friends. It had been the Metamorphia's stronghold, and Daltec was studying the tablets he had uncovered there, trying to find anything that would help defeat Zuba once and for all. Nolan suppressed a shudder as he thought of their enemy. She was still out there somewhere in Tangala, doubtless up to no good.

"In that case, I'll see you all later," Rotu said, striding quickly away. Marilla had set down her ham bone and was staring after the prince, her gold-flecked eyes uneasy. Nolan suddenly felt unsettled too.

"What is it?" Nolan asked Marilla.

"*I'm not sure...*" the wolf answered.

"Probably nothing. I've never met the prince before. But something about him smelled...unnatural."

At that moment, a horn blared in the courtyard outside – three quick blasts, followed by a long one. An icy chill washed over Nolan, followed by a rush of heat. That signal was special – it was only blown on the regent's return. Yet Rotu was already present, wasn't he? Nolan leapt up and hurried to the window, where Marilla quickly joined him. Outside, Prince Rotu was just dismounting from his horse, met by two members of the palace guard.

Nolan and Marilla shared a horrified glance. Whoever they had just directed to Daltec's study, it hadn't been the prince at all!

NEVER GIVE UP

Nolan and Marilla raced from the room, followed closely by Katya, Miandra and Rafe along with their mystical companions. They all hurried up the spiral stairs that led to Daltec's study, right at the top of a turret. As he climbed the

tower, taking the stairs two at a time, Nolan could hear crashes and bangs from above him. His stomach twisted with dread.

The crashes got louder as they neared Daltec's room and now Nolan could hear glass breaking, and the ***THUMP*** of heavy objects being shifted. Faint flashes of blue and green light flickered across the staircase walls, and as Nolan rounded the last bend, he saw that the light was coming from beneath the door to Daltec's chamber. Nolan tugged at the handle, but the door was locked. From inside the room he heard a terrible, wordless cry that chilled him to the bone. The cry was suddenly cut short, followed by a heavy ***THUD***. *Daltec!*

"Let us in!" Nolan cried, as his friends and their companions all crowded on to the landing around him. "Are you all right?"

"Mind out of the way," Rafe said, his huge, heavy hammer drawn back over his shoulder. Nolan moved aside, and Rafe slammed his hammer into the wood of the door, just above the lock. The door crashed inwards, and Nolan bustled after Rafe into the room. Chaos greeted them. Bottles and vials lay smashed all over the floor, their bright contents spilled over strewn papers and scrolls. Daltec's desk had been overturned and all the drawers pulled out, their contents scattered. But far worse, Nolan could see Daltec's boots sticking out from behind his upturned desk. And perched above the fallen wizard was Zuba, crouching on the windowsill, her hood thrown back and her face twisted into an evil sneer.

“What have you done to him?” Miandra demanded, levelling the prongs of her trident at the sorceress.

“He’s not dead,” Zuba crowed, her black eyes filled with mirth. “Although he may as well be. I’ve taught him a valuable lesson: not to mess with magic he doesn’t understand.”

“You will pay for this!” Miandra cried, lunging across the room towards Zuba, aiming her trident at the sorceress’s chest. With a cocky wave, Zuba tipped backwards, toppling from the windowsill and vanishing from sight. Nolan raced to the sill, quickly followed by Miandra and the others. He half expected to see Zuba's lifeless body spread on the cobbles below, but instead, he saw a giant vulture flapping away on broad wings. Miandra aimed her trident again, as if to throw it at the bird, but Nolan could see the creature was too far away. The vulture gave a triumphant shriek before quickly becoming a dark and distant speck among the clouds.

Nolan turned back to the room to see Katya kneeling at Daltec's side, gripping the wizard's limp hand. Daltec's eyes were open a crack, but only the whites showed.

"He's breathing, but barely," Katya said. "We have to help him!"

"How?" Miandra asked. Nolan felt sicker than ever, the food he had eaten forming a cold, hard knot in his stomach. The only person with the skills to help Daltec was the young wizard himself.

Marilla had been sniffing through the contents of Daltec's upturned desk, as if searching for something. Now she turned to Nolan, her eyes filled with worry. "*The purple jewels we brought back with us are gone,*" she told Nolan. "*Zuba must have taken them.*"

Nolan's shoulders sagged. "After everything we've done, Zuba's still one step ahead of us!" he said.

Rafe nodded miserably. "What's the good of defeating Beasts if we can't help Daltec?" he said.

"And without Daltec, we can't hope to stop Zuba," Miandra added.

Katya hung her head, looking as wretched and defeated as Nolan felt. "All our efforts have been for nothing!" she said, bitterly.

Taking in the weary, sorrowful

gazes of his friends, Nolan was about to agree. But then he noticed something. They all looked far older than when they had first met, and stronger too – the weight of a kingdom resting on their shoulders. Each one of them would give their life to help Daltec, or to defend Tangala. Nolan balled his fists, and drew himself up tall.

"Not for nothing!" he said. "We have all proved ourselves on our Quests. We can't lose hope now. Tom and Elenna never did. If we work together, we can find a cure for Daltec, and we will stop Zuba too,

whatever she has planned." He held out his hand towards Rafe, palm down. Rafe hesitated for a moment, but then he too straightened his spine and put his hand on top of Nolan's. Marilla raised a paw, setting it on Rafe's hand, and Katya joined them, followed by Veradu. Soon, all four New Protectors and their companions were standing in a tight ring, shoulder to shoulder. A surge of determination warmed Nolan's blood.

"For Tangala!" Nolan cried.

"For Tangala!" his friends replied, their voices ringing out together, filled with unity and new resolve.

THE END

CONGRATULATIONS, YOU HAVE COMPLETED THIS QUEST!

At the end of each chapter you were awarded a special gold coin. The QUEST in this book was worth an amazing 8 coins.

Look at the Beast Quest totem picture opposite to see how far you've come in your journey to become

MASTER OF THE BEASTS.

The more books you read, the more coins you will collect!

Do you want your own Beast Quest Totem?

1. Cut out and collect the coin below
2. Go to the Beast Quest website
3. Download and print out your totem
4. Add your coin to the totem

www.beastquest.co.uk

READ THE BOOKS, COLLECT THE COINS!

EARN COINS FOR EVERY CHAPTER YOU READ!

550+
515
480
445
410
395
380
365
350
320
290
260
230
217
206
191
180
146
112
78
44
30
19
8

550+ COINS
MASTER OF THE BEASTS

410 COINS
HERO

350 COINS
WARRIOR

230 COINS
KNIGHT

180 COINS
SQUIRE

44 COINS
PAGE

8 COINS
APPRENTICE

READ ALL THE BOOKS IN SERIES 31:

GUARDIANS

OF TANGALA

ADAM BLADE
Beast Quest
HERAXOR
THE FIRE HAWK

ADAM BLADE
Beast Quest
PETROK
THE STONE WARRIOR

Don't miss the first book in this exciting Beast Quest series: Lupix the Ice Wolf! Read on for a sneak peek...

THE FORGOTTEN CITY

"Well, it's official," muttered Katya. "That wizard is a few powders short of a potion."

Rafe stifled a laugh, in spite of everything. His boots were waterlogged; his tunic hung damp and heavy from his shoulders. *And it's still raining!*

The New Protectors had been trudging through the forest for hours. Daltec strode ahead, leading the way. He seemed tireless, moving fast, his nose buried in the sodden old map he had brought with him.

Where in the name of Aroha is he taking us?

They had given up asking the wizard himself. He was too absorbed in his own thoughts to answer.

Rafe brushed past dripping ferns

and stumbled over a tree root. His boots squelched in sludgy mud. The forest seemed to be getting thicker and darker the further they went. Raindrops pattered on the leafy canopy overhead, but every now and then a big droplet found its way through and drenched him further.

He stumbled again, and his golden-headed hammer swung halfway off his shoulder.

"Whoa!" The weapon was so heavy it almost tipped him over. But he was glad to have it with him, all the same. *Who knows what creatures might lurk in this forest?*

"This isn't what we signed up for!" groaned Nolan. "We're supposed to be fighting Evil, not hiking through marshland!" He looked miserable, just like the others.

Rafe thought of their mentor, Tom, who had bestowed some of the power of his own Golden Armour upon their weapons. What would the great Avantian hero say? "I'm sure Daltec knows what he's doing," said Rafe, trying to sound cheerful.

"Right," said Miandra, rolling her eyes. "He looks *exactly* like someone who knows what they're doing."

Daltec had stopped again, peering

at the map, his pointy hat drooping in the rain. "It has to be here..." the wizard muttered to himself.

"Let's just ask him one more time," said Rafe, starting forward. "Daltec? Where—"

His foot smacked into something and he fell, sprawling in the mud. *Urgh!* He was plastered in the stuff.

He sat up, smearing muck from his hands on to his tunic. "Hey," he spluttered. "Is this a wall?"

The other three young heroes clustered round to see what Rafe had tripped over. It was tumbledown and ruined; the stones were set unevenly and hidden by the undergrowth. But there was no doubt about it.

"Someone actually *lived* out here?" said Nolan, with a shudder.

They were startled by a wild whoop of triumph. Rafe gasped to see Daltec dancing with joy, tossing his hat in the air and catching it again. “Well done, Rafe!” he cried. “You’ve found it!”

“Found what?” Rafe asked the wizard, quite baffled.

“Why, the fabled city, of course! The great stronghold of Saitang!”

“Er...stronghold?” said Katya doubtfully, looking round at the dense knot of trees and vegetation on all sides.

“*Ancient* stronghold,” said Daltec. “Ruined centuries ago.” His eyes sparkled as he darted through the mud, tracing the line of the wall. “This way! Quickly!”

Rafe staggered to his feet,

brushing himself down as he followed the others. They could hardly keep up with the wizard.

"Saitang!" Daltec was saying. "No doubt you've heard of it? Tangala's imperial capital! Or rather, it *was*, a thousand years ago." He stopped suddenly. "There! Impressive, no?"

Rafe felt a shiver of astonishment pass through him as he gazed upwards. They had come out into a clearing, where a dilapidated building had been hidden by the trees. It was a tall tower, roughly built of pale stone and covered with moss.

There was something strangely sad about seeing such a building here, alone and abandoned, with only the forest for company.

"Behold...a relic from the Age of Magic," said Daltec, his voice hushed with awe.

"The age of what, now?" panted Katya.

Daltec huffed. "The time of the Metamorphia, of course!"

Metamorphia... The word stirred an uneasy memory for Rafe. "The Metamorphia are sorcerers, aren't they?" he said, slowly. "Isn't Zuba one of them?"

The air seemed to turn chilly at the very mention of the witch. She had done her worst, trying to destroy the kingdom. *And to think she's still out there, somewhere. Plotting her revenge...*

"I'm afraid so," said Daltec. "The Metamorphia were once the most respected sorcerers in Tangala. That is, until they defied the Emperor. They used their magic to fuse humans with Beasts and create new life – magical Guardians to defend Tangala. After that, they were all but erased from the annals."

"So how do *you* know about them?" asked Nolan.

"The Circle of Wizards keeps records of the enemies of all kingdoms," said Daltec proudly.

"But why did you bring *us* here?"

said Miandra, one eyebrow raised.

"Allow me to show you." Daltec flexed his fingers, and a soft blue light flickered around them. The wizard carefully moulded the magical light into a ball. Then, with a thrust of his hands, he sent it darting up to the top of the tower. There, the light dispersed, creating a shimmering blue haze.

Read

LUPIX THE ICE WOLF

to find out what happens next!

Don't miss this thrilling series from Adam Blade!